W9-ASI-524

ON THE RUN

by H. Townson

Illustrated by Brann Garvey

Librarian Reviewer
Kathleen Baxter
Children's Literature Consultant
formerly with Anoka County Library, MN
BA College of Saint Catherine, St. Paul, MN
MA in Library Science, University of Minnesota

Reading Consultant
Elizabeth Stedem
Educator/Consultant, Colorado Springs, CO
MA in Elementary Education, University of Denver, CO

STONE ARCH BOOKS
MINNEAPOLIS   SAN DIEGO

j
TOW

First published in the United States in 2007
by Stone Arch Books,
151 Good Counsel Drive, P.O. Box 669,
Mankato, Minnesota 56002.
www.stonearchbooks.com

Published by arrangement with
Barrington Stoke Ltd, Edinburgh.

Copyright © 2002 Hazel Townson

The right of Hazel Townson to be identified as the author
of this work has been asserted by her in accordance
with the Copyright, Designs and Patent Act 1988.

All rights reserved. No part of this publication may be reproduced
in whole or in part, or stored in a retrieval system, or transmitted in any
form or by any means, electronic, mechanical, photocopying, recording,
or otherwise, without written permission of the publisher.

Library of Congress Cataloging-in-Publication Data
Townson, Hazel.
    On the Run / by H. Townson; illustrated by Brann Garvey.
    p. cm. — (Pathway Books)
    Summary: Ronnie hates sports and always gets out of them one way
or another, but when he pretends to be sick to avoid Sports Day at school,
Ronnie encounters something much more frightening than the high jump or
tug-of-war.
    ISBN-13: 978-1-59889-105-8 (hardcover)
    ISBN-10: 1-59889-105-7 (hardcover)
    ISBN-13: 978-1-59889-262-8 (paperback)
    ISBN-10: 1-59889-262-2 (paperback)
    [1. Sports—Fiction. 2. Burglary—Fiction. 3. Schools—Fiction.]
I. Garvey, Brann, ill. II. Title. III. Series.
PZ7.T6675On 2007
[Fic]—dc22   2006007177

Art Director: Heather Kindseth
Cover Graphic Designer: Brann Garvey
Interior Graphic Designer: Kay Fraser

1 2 3 4 5 6 11 10 09 08 07 06

Printed in the United States of America

TABLE OF CONTENTS

CHAPTER 1

A TERRIBLE MISTAKE

Ronnie hated all sports. He knew he could kick, catch, run, and jump better than anyone else, but why bother? It was too much like hard work.

Let other kids chase a ball and then stumble home with mud all over them. Ronnie thought it was more fun to watch TV.

If anyone said he was lazy, he would just laugh. Let them think that. Ronnie knew he wasn't lazy. He was just wise. After all, you wouldn't see him limping home from a game, all wet and worn out.

Tuesdays and Fridays were Ronnie's bad days because there were sports at school all afternoon. He always found a good excuse not to join in. Sometimes he had a bad back, or he had hay fever, or a dentist's appointment.

But there was one thing Ronnie couldn't get out of, and that was his school's Sports Day.

No one could get out of Sports Day. The principal made sure every student joined in on Sports Day every year.

There were all kinds of races, games, and contests to choose. Ronnie always ended up doing tug-of-war because he wouldn't join any other teams.

But not this year!

When Ronnie looked down the lists for Sports Day, he was amazed to find his name wasn't on them.

A new gym teacher had just started. His name was Mr. Springer.

He must have drawn up the lists for Sports Day in such a hurry that he had forgotten Ronnie.

How lucky could he be? Ronnie knew he should tell Mr. Springer, but he wasn't going to.

Ronnie figured no one would notice that he was not on the list. Everyone would be too busy to figure it out. People said that the principal had so much work to do, he might not even come to Sports Day.

Never trust what people say! The principal was not going to miss Sports Day. He knew the names of all the students. Three days before Sports Day, the principal looked at the lists with Mr. Springer. Right away, he noticed that Ronnie's name was missing.

"Didn't Ronnie come and tell you that he wasn't on any list?" the principal asked Mr. Springer. "He knows that everybody joins in on Sports Day. Everybody!"

"He hasn't said anything to me yet," replied Mr. Springer.

The principal frowned. "Well, he's had lots of time to talk to you about it. I bet he's trying to get out of it. We ought to make him do the high jump!"

The principal just meant Ronnie deserved a tough event for trying to get out of Sports Day. But before he could explain, he was called away. Mr. Springer thought that the principal really wanted Ronnie to do the high jump, so he added Ronnie's name to the list.

Things were looking bad for Ronnie, as bad as they could be.

CHAPTER 2

ONE JUMP AHEAD

That afternoon, when Mr. Springer told him he had to do the high jump, Ronnie couldn't hide his shock.

"But sir, I can't jump! I, um, I've got a funny heel," he said.

Mr. Springer looked at Ronnie's feet.

"They look okay to me. Have you ever tried the high jump?" he asked.

"Well, no, sir. But I wouldn't be any good. I'm just not that type, sir."

"If the principal thinks you can do it, then you have to try," Mr. Springer told him. "Meet me at the track at 8:30 tomorrow morning. You can try it out."

Ronnie knew the high jump was no joke. In fact, it was very hard work. He'd have to train for it. What a drag!

"I can't get to school by 8:30. My bus doesn't get here till 8:50," said Ronnie.

"Then you'll have to walk or catch a city bus that does get here on time," replied Mr. Springer.

"My mom won't let me walk because I might get run over," Ronnie told him.

"Oh, come on. Your mom will be proud that you're on the team. And you should be proud that the principal thinks you can do it," said Mr. Springer.

"You don't want to let us all down, do you?" he asked. "Come to school at 8:30 tomorrow. That's an order."

"Yes, sir," said Ronnie.

When Mr. Springer saw that Ronnie was upset, he added, "You don't know what you can do until you try. And I'll be there to help you."

It was the worst day of Ronnie's life. He'd been caught. Even worse, if his parents found out that he was on the high jump team, they would come to Sports Day!

When Ronnie got home, he felt sick about it. His parents were not back from work yet. Ronnie let himself into the house. How could he get out of this bad dream? He felt sick. Sick?

Ronnie knew what he had to do. He would stay home from school the next day!

He would be sick. And he'd be sick again the next day. And the day after that, which was Sports Day. He could write out an excuse for his teacher in his mom's handwriting.

He felt fine now. Why hadn't he thought of this before? He had never skipped school like other kids sometimes did. Why not now?

Ronnie began to make plans. He would set out for school, but not get on the bus. He couldn't just hang around the streets. His dad was a delivery truck driver and might drive by at any moment. It would be better to slip back home after his parents left for work.

Ronnie sat down at his desk to write the note. He didn't like lying, but he was desperate.

He tried again and again to write like his mom, but it wasn't working. He tore all the notes into shreds. Then he had an idea.

He found his mom's shopping list. Now he could copy the way she wrote each letter.

"Ronnie will not be at school today. He is sick," he wrote, and signed his mother's name.

He put the note in an envelope and addressed it to his teacher.

I solved that problem, thought Ronnie. He felt happy again.

How wrong he was.

CHAPTER 3

ENTER — A BURGLAR!

The next day, Ronnie got ready for school the way he always did.

"Watch out for the traffic, honey!" his mother warned him as she left for work.

"Come on, son, I'll give you a lift," joked Ronnie's dad, starting up his delivery truck.

Ronnie's dad knew that his son would rather die than be seen getting a ride to school in his dad's truck.

Ronnie waved goodbye and headed toward the bus stop as his dad drove off the other way.

He hurried to the stop, gave the envelope to a classmate, and told him that he was staying home sick.

He knew his friend would deliver the note. Now Ronnie was all set for a relaxing day at home.

He didn't want to be seen walking back home, so he took a shortcut.

He ran through a neighbor's yard, jumped over a small hedge, and let himself in the back door. No one saw him.

He thought maybe it would be okay to skip school if he spent the day working on his Save the Earth project for science class.

He sat down at his desk and began to write an outline for his project.

After a while, he started to get bored. The morning dragged on and soon he felt hungry.

He went downstairs to the kitchen.

The first thing he saw on the kitchen table was his dad's newspaper.

The headline on the front page screamed BURGLAR KIDNAPS BOY in big, black letters.

Ronnie snatched up the paper and began to read.

The boy in the story was named Sam. He lived in the very next town. That made the story even scarier.

While Sam's parents were out, Sam came home and found a burglar in the house.

The burglar tried to grab Sam and drive away with him in a green van.

Had they found the burglar yet? Ronnie wanted to read on and find out, but just then there was a lot of noise outside the front door.

Thump, drag, thump, drag.

He put down the newspaper to listen. It was too early for the mailman, so who could it be?

Ronnie waited for the doorbell to ring. Horror of horrors — it could be someone from school!

It was even worse than that. Ronnie could now hear a key turn in the lock.

Someone was coming in!

Ronnie was in a panic. It must be one of his parents. They couldn't see that he stayed home!

Quick as a wink, he hid in the closet under the stairs, where the boots were kept.

For a time, he hunched in the dark among the boots and listened.

Someone was stomping up and down the hall, making a lot of noise. It didn't sound like his mom or dad.

Ronnie had to know who it was. He opened the closet door a crack and peeked out.

He was just in time to see a stranger walking down the hall.

The man was carrying the family's
TV set.

Beyond the open front door, Ronnie
saw a green van parked right outside
the house.

A green van!

What did it say in the newspaper? The burglar who surprised Sam had a green van.

This man in the hall, this burglar who was taking their TV, must be the same one.

He might try to kidnap Ronnie too if he saw him!

Ronnie felt sick and dizzy. He fell against the closet door and it swung open with a crash.

The burglar turned around, and Ronnie saw right into his startled eyes.

It would be better to face the high jump than this burglar. Ronnie thought he would remember this moment for the rest of his life. If he still had a life.

The burglar didn't have a mask over his face.

This scared Ronnie. The man must have been very sure that he would get away with it.

If anyone saw the burglar, they would think he was taking the TV to repair it. They wouldn't call the police or rush to help Ronnie. Even though Ronnie might soon be gone.

Ronnie and the burglar had stared at each other, eye to eye. Now the burglar knows that I have seen his face, thought Ronnie.

He knows I'll remember it, too. How can I ever forget it?

It makes me enemy number one!

He'll have to shut me up, just like he did with that boy, Sam.

Before the man could grab him, Ronnie crashed out of the back door and fled.

#
NO HIDING PLACE

Ronnie was sure the burglar would follow him.

The burglar did have his arms full with the TV, but he would soon get rid of that. Then he could chase him in that green van.

Better keep off the roads. Ronnie ran straight to the park.

Okay so far, but he couldn't stay in the park all day.

He didn't want to go and tell his parents or the police. If he did, they'd find out that he didn't go to school.

There must be somewhere he could hide until the end of the school day. Then he could go home late.

He would make sure that he arrived after his mom. He wanted her to be the one to find out that the TV was gone.

By that time, thought Ronnie, the burglar will know that I haven't told on him. So he won't need to follow me after all.

But where could he hide right now? He would have to find a good place. It was a matter of life or death.

Then Ronnie thought of something he learned at school.

If you hid in a church, no one could come in and get you.

He ran over to St. Steven's, but the church door was locked.

Just my luck, thought Ronnie.

He turned away. Then he saw the library. He could hide in there. No one got kidnapped in a library.

The children's library was always busy when Ronnie went there after school.

Now it was almost empty.

Mrs. Oates, the librarian, was sitting at her desk.

Ronnie could see that she had her eye on him.

He fled to the back of the room, grabbed an old book, and pretended to read it.

That did not stop Mrs. Oates from coming over to talk to him.

"Why aren't you in school?" she asked.

"I'm, uh, working on my Save the Earth project," Ronnie told her.

Mrs. Oates looked at his book. "Well, you won't get much help from a book on ballet dancing."

Ronnie blushed and said nothing. He was no good at lying.

"Did your teacher send you here?" asked Mrs. Oates.

"We, um, I have to find things out for myself," Ronnie told her.

He knew that it was a mistake to go to the library.

He put the book on a shelf and ran out of the door.

Now where should he go? It had started to rain.

Blame Sports Day!

Blame Mr. Springer and the principal! They were the ones who got him into this mess.

CHAPTER 5

ONE SHOCK AFTER ANOTHER!

The rain was pouring down, and Ronnie needed to find shelter.

He could go to the shopping center. Ronnie usually loved going there.

He liked hunting for dropped coins. He once found two dollars' worth in a single day!

But the shopping center was a long way away. Plus, it was near the school.

Ronnie was still afraid that someone might spot him. He had to be very careful.

He kept looking back, but he didn't see a sign of the green van.

By the time he got to the shopping center, he was sure the burglar had lost track of him.

Whew!

Ronnie was wet, so he didn't want to sit down on a bench and get it all wet, too.

He ducked into the toy store and stood in a corner, hoping to get dry.

He still felt shaky, but safe and much more hopeful. A green van could not drive in here.

He started to think of himself as kind of a hero. After all, he escaped from a burglar who wanted to kidnap him.

Life isn't over yet, Ronnie thought.

He began to look around. Right in front of him, he saw a new type of model airplane on the shelf.

Ronnie was interested in model planes. He picked it up. Just as he was looking at the price and figuring out how long it would take him to save up for it, someone grabbed his arm.

"Hey there," said the store owner, "I've been watching you. You were about to steal that plane, weren't you? Well, get back to school!"

What a shock! How could the owner think he was going to steal the model plane? He had never stolen anything. He had only picked up lost coins, and that wasn't the same thing.

"I was just looking," Ronnie said.

"That's what they all say. You can come back after school and have a good look then," said the owner.

The owner took the plane from Ronnie and pushed him out of the shop.

Ronnie ran off. What an insult!

"Watch where you're going!" a woman yelled as he ran right into her.

"Kids!" said her friend in disgust. "No manners at all! And why isn't he in school?"

Ronnie took off again.

Just as he jumped over a bench, he spotted a man putting a TV set in a shop window. It looked just like his family's TV.

Ronnie stopped and looked at the sign above the window. It said, **Get Your Almost New TVs, Radios, and Stereos Here**.

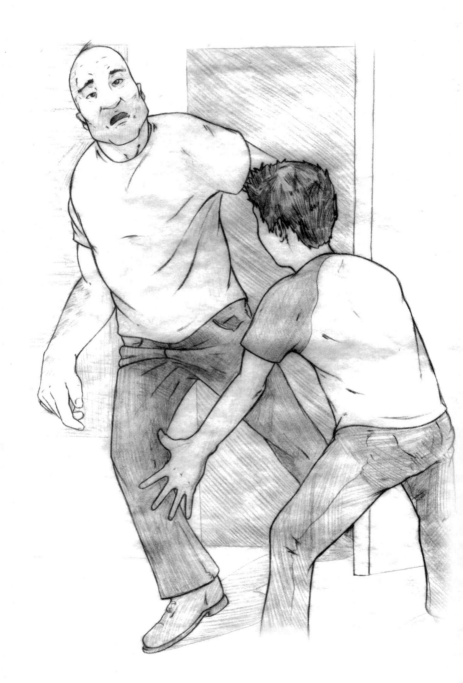

Ronnie looked hard at the TV set. He knew it was his because it had a scratch on the side.

So the burglar came into the shopping center! Maybe he was here right now, waiting to grab him.

Ronnie looked around in panic.

The place was packed with people. Ronnie thought that he could never forget the burglar's face.

But as he looked around, he knew that any of the men around him could be the burglar.

That was it! He would have to tell the police while the TV was still in the window.

If he waited, the TV might be sold.

Once the TV was gone, no one would believe his story.

There was a pay phone near the toy shop. He could dial 911 for free. Ronnie spun around to run back to it, and came face to face with the burglar!

CHAPTER 6

A LEAP FOR DEAR LIFE

Ronnie had never run so fast. He dashed in and out between people. It was amazing what you could do when your life was at risk.

Once he thought he saw the burglar's reflection in a store window. This made him run even faster.

Soon he was outside the shopping center and rushing down Hill Street toward school.

Toward school?

He no longer cared about being found out.

School was the safest place to be. Even the principal wouldn't stand by and let him get kidnapped.

Ronnie had to get there as soon as he could.

Hill Street was steep and the school was at the bottom, beyond the track and playing fields.

The ground was wet and slippery from the rain.

Ronnie ran faster and faster. As he shot down the hill it became clear that he could not stop himself.

What could he do?

All around the playing fields were high hedges. There were two gates in the hedge, but they were a long way off.

Ronnie found himself rushing straight toward the hedge.

The hedge was almost four feet high, but Ronnie made a giant leap and flew right over it!

He landed on the grass of the playing field a few yards from Mr. Springer, the gym teacher.

Mr. Springer was amazed.

Ronnie lay panting on the grass. Mr. Springer rushed over to make sure Ronnie was okay. Then he helped him to his feet.

"Well, I'm sorry you didn't get to school this morning as we planned. But now we know that you can jump as well as anyone, and better than most people," Mr. Springer said.

If anyone could save Ronnie now, it was Mr. Springer.

Ronnie took a deep breath and began to tell his story.

"Someone is trying to kidnap me!" said Ronnie. "He's been chasing me all around the shopping center. I'm sure he's still after me. That's why I jumped over the hedge."

"Oh, my," Mr. Springer said. "That's the worst excuse for not coming to school that I've ever heard."

"Honest, sir, he stole our TV. I saw him," said Ronnie. "That's why he's chasing me," he added. "He already kidnapped a boy named Sam. And he's driving a green van."

"Now, now, no more excuses from you," said Mr. Springer. "I think you stayed away from school because you didn't want to try the high jump." He shook his head.

"Well, you'd better come for training after school today, Ronnie," added Mr. Springer. "You're a born jumper."

"But, but, sir," said Ronnie.

"Don't say another word, Ronnie. Get back to your classroom, and be thankful that I'm not going to tell your silly excuse to the principal," said Mr. Springer.

CHAPTER 7

A BIG SURPRISE

Ronnie crossed the playing field to go to his classroom. He thought he'd be safe from the burglar once he was back in school. But what would he tell his teacher?

Then he spotted a delivery truck outside the gym door.

It was his dad's truck! His dad was bringing some new benches for the school.

Ronnie started to run.

"Dad! Dad! Wait for me!" he yelled, as his father walked back to his truck.

Here at last was someone who would believe Ronnie's story, even if it did get him into trouble.

"There's a burglar, Dad! And he's trying to kidnap me!" Ronnie said.

"What's all this?" his dad said with a laugh.

"It's true, Dad!"

Ronnie's dad could see that his son was really upset. He put an arm around his shoulder.

"Okay, just calm down, and take it slowly, son. Where was this burglar? At school?" asked his dad.

"No, at our house! This burglar stole our TV, and he has a green van, and he probably would have killed me. It says so right in your newspaper," Ronnie said.

"Our TV?" Dad asked.

Ronnie's dad began to laugh again. "If you mean Jack Briggs, he took our old TV and put in a new one. It was going to be a surprise for you and Mom. Wait until you see it!"

He clapped his hands together. "Ronnie, it's great. Wide screen, high definition. You'll love it. I gave Jack a key to the house, so he could get it set up before Mom and you got home."

Then Dad looked puzzled. "Wait a minute. How did you know about it, anyway? You were at school."

Here it comes, thought Ronnie.

But his father was going to find out one way or another, so Ronnie told him the whole story.

"But how could I know it was Jack Briggs, not a burglar, who was out to get me?" Ronnie asked. "He was chasing me, Dad!"

"He must have seen how scared you were and wanted to tell you who he was. Or he thought *you* were a burglar when you ran off like that," Dad explained. "I hope you've learned your lesson. It doesn't pay to skip school."

Ronnie found it hard to take all this in. He felt angry. Someone had made a fool out of him.

But there was one good thing about all this. Dad would see that Ronnie was too shaken up to train for Sports Day. Dad would get him out of it.

No such luck!

Mr. Springer came over just then to see why Ronnie hadn't gone back to his class. Dad told him who he was. He also told Mr. Springer what Ronnie just told him. "He got it all wrong," Dad said, "but you can see the boy's upset."

Ronnie thought Mr. Springer would say that none of this would have happened if Ronnie had come to school this morning. But that's not what he said.

All he could talk about was finding out that Ronnie was a star at the high jump. He told Dad how Ronnie came racing down the hill, and how he leaped over the hedge.

"It was one of the best jumps I've ever seen," said Mr. Springer. "And with training, he'll be even better."

Ronnie's dad grinned. "I always knew he had it in him," he said with pride. "Just wait until I tell his mom that Ronnie might win the high jump on Sports Day."

"But Dad, you can't be serious, after all that's happened to me today," cried Ronnie in a panic.

His dad did not seem to hear. He was thinking of the moment when Ronnie would win the high jump.

Then Dad had an idea. "Tell you what," he said to Mr. Springer, "since Ronnie ran down that hill so fast, why don't you put him in the hundred-meter dash as well? I bet he can win that, too. I'll see you on Sports Day!"

ABOUT THE AUTHOR

When Hazel Townson was a librarian, she found
that a lot of children were struggling to read the
books they had borrowed. She decided she should
write stories they would enjoy and understand.
Now she's a full-time writer. She lives in England,
and is the author of many books for children.

ABOUT THE ILLUSTRATOR

Brann Garvey grew up in the great state of Iowa,
where he studied art and visual communications.
He graduated from the Minneapolis College of
Art and Design with a degree in illustration.
Brann is usually found with one or more of the
following: a pencil in his hand, a comic book, a
remote for watching DVDs, or his pet kitty, Iggy.
When the weather is nice, Brann likes to play
disc golf, and he proudly points out that Iowa is
one of the world's centers for the sport. Iggy does
not play.

GLOSSARY

ballet (bal-LAY)—a style of dance

burglar (BURG-lur)—someone who breaks into a building and steals things

delivery (di-LIV-ur-ee)—taking something to someone

desperate (DESS-pur-it)—willing to do anything to change your situation

hedge (HEJ)—a row of bushes planted to form a wall

shreds (SHREDZ)—pieces of something that has been torn

startled (STAR-tuhld)—surprised or frightened

type (TIPE)—a specific kind of a person or thing

DISCUSSION QUESTIONS

1. Ronnie decides to skip school in order to get out of Sports Day. Did you think his plan would work? Why or why not?

2. Mr. Springer is a new gym teacher who doesn't know Ronnie very well. In what ways do you think Mr. Springer is a good teacher?

3. Why do you think Ronnie's dad is happy about the high jump? Why does he want Ronnie to run the 100-yard dash as well?

WRITING PROMPTS

1. BURGLAR KIDNAPS BOY, the headline says. Pretend you are a reporter and write the first paragraph of the newspaper story about Sam and the real burglar.

2. Write about a time when you felt like skipping school to get out of something. How did it work out?

3. Ronnie doesn't want to train for the high jump, but somehow he spends his whole day running and jumping. Write a list of the places Ronnie ran and jumped on the day he tried to skip school.

ALSO BY
H. TOWNSON

The Secret Room

Adam suddenly finds himself in a very different world, one in which he could be in terrible danger.

ALSO PUBLISHED BY STONE ARCH BOOKS

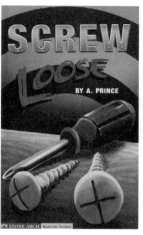

Screw Loose
A. Prince

Max finds a screwdriver on the way home from school. Suddenly, he has a tool that will make the entire school fall apart. The real question is: will he be able to put it back together before he becomes unhinged?

Bungee Hero
J. Bertagna

Adam is terrified riding Mr. Vertigo's Big Ferris Wheel at the local carnival. He is tired of being afraid, so he plans to overcome his fear of heights in an extreme way — bungee jumping.

INTERNET SITES

Do you want to know more about subjects related to this book? Or are you interested in learning about other topics? Then check out FactHound, a fun, easy way to find Internet sites.

Our investigative staff has already sniffed out great sites for you!

Here's how to use FactHound:

1. Visit *www.facthound.com*

2. Select your grade level.

3. To learn more about subjects related to this book, type in the book's ISBN number: **1598891057**.

4. Click the **Fetch It** button.

FactHound will fetch the best Internet sites for you!